Cat's *Adventure*

in Alphabet Town

by *Laura Alden*
illustrated by *Jodie McCallum*

created by Wing Park Publishers

CHILDRENS PRESS ®
CHICAGO

Library of Congress Cataloging-in-Publication Data

Alden, Laura, 1955-
     Cat's Adventure in Alphabet Town / by Laura Alden ;
illustrated by Jodie McCallum.
          p.   cm. — (Read around Alphabet Town)
     Summary: Cat meets "c" words on her adventure in Alphabet
Town. Includes activities.
     ISBN 0-516-05403-1
     [1. Alphabet—Fiction.   2. Cats—Fiction.]   I. McCallum, Jodie,
ill.   II. Title.   III. Series.
PZ7.A3586Cat   1992
[E]—dc 20   91-3605
                                                                                CIP

Cat's *Adventure*

in Alphabet Town

You are now entering Alphabet Town,
With houses from "A" to "Z."
I'm going on a "C" adventure today,
So come along with me.

This is the "C" house of Alphabet Town. Cat lives here.

Cat likes everything that begins
with the letter ''c.'' She likes
to color.

And she likes to climb,

but not too high.

Today Cat and her cousin are going to the carnival in Alphabet Town.

Cat wears her new

cowboy hat.

"Cool," says her cousin.

The two cats hurry to the carnival.
They climb over a fence and see

clowns!

The clowns are wearing costumes.
One clown plays the

clarinet.

Cat dances with the clowns.

"Cool," says her cousin.

Next Cat sees a big

camera.

Cat and her cousin hurry over.
They smile and say, "Cookies."
"Click" goes the camera.

Then the two cats walk around a corner and see tables full of

coconut cakes, custard pies,

cookies and candy!

They buy two pieces of coconut cake, two pieces of custard pie, and lots of cookies and candy.

They eat everything, except for a few

crumbs.

Next they meet some friends at the carnival. "Hey, look!" says Cat.

"Here comes

Calf   and   Cow

and   Camel."

Then they all go to see the carnival rides. "Let's ride in the bumper cars," calls Cat.

All the animals climb into the cars and...

CRASH!

The cars go fast, then slow, then CRASH again.

At last, the cars stop. The carnival is closed for the day.

Cat and her cousin climb back over
the fence and go home.

Cat is tired. She hangs up her
cowboy hat.

Then she climbs into bed and crawls under the covers.

Soon Cat is asleep. She dreams about clowns, costumes, crowds and cars.

And one more piece of coconut cake.

MORE FUN WITH CAT

What's in a Name?

In my "c" adventure, you read many "c" words. My name begins with a "C." Many of my friends' names begin with "C" too. Here are a few.

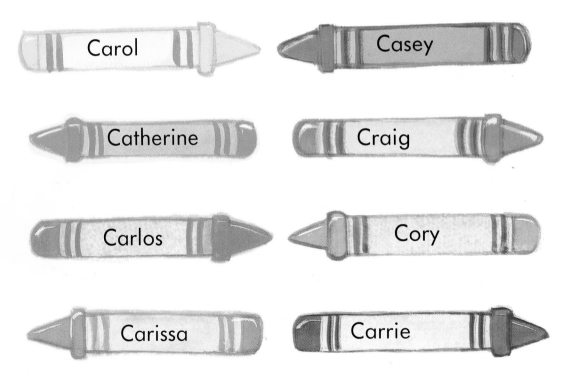

Carol

Casey

Catherine

Craig

Carlos

Cory

Carissa

Carrie

Can you think of other names that begin with "C"?
Does your name begin with "C"?

Cat's Word Hunt

I like to hunt for words with "c" in them. Can you help me find the words on this page that begin with "c"? How many are there? Can you read them?

apple

car

bacon

sock

cup

candle

bucket

truck

Can you find any words with "ck" at the end?
Can you find any with "c" in the middle?
Can you find a word with no "c"?

Cat's Favorite Things

"C" is my favorite letter. I love "c" things. Can you guess why? You can find some of my favorite "c" things in my house on page 7. How many "c" things can you find there? Can you think of more "c" things?

Now you make up a "c" adventure.